Usborne
Little Stickers
Farm

Illustrated by
Louisa Boyles

Words by Jessica Greenwell
Designed by Kirsty Tizzard
and Maddison Warnes

You'll find all the
stickers at the back
of the book.

In the farmyard

The farmyard is a busy place. Can you add all the people, animals, tractors and trucks to this picture?

Find a place to park the tractor.

Stick some horses
in the stalls.

Add a gate and the
farm name here.

At the cowshed

The cows wake up early with the sun and
a noisy rooster calls, "cock-adoodle-dooo!"

Fill the picture with
cows and calves.

Stick on the farmer feeding
some hungry cows.

Stick some cows in the cowshed.

5

Lots of sheep

The sheep and the lambs in the meadow graze on the grass and snooze in the sunshine.

Add some more sheep to the picture.

Find a friendly sheepdog to look after the sheep.

At the pig pen

Pigs love muddy puddles. The piglets are very playful, all splashing and snorting noisily.

Find a spot for some pigs eating from their trough.

Stick some playful piglets in the mud.

At the pond

The farm's pond is home to lots of animals and insects. Can you add them all to the picture?

Stick on a frog hopping off this rock.

Fill the pond with ducks and ducklings.

Hens and chicks

Hens lay eggs inside the henhouse, and the farmer collects them every day. Stick on all the hens, chicks and eggs.

Find a place for a basket of eggs.

How many chicks can you find to add to the picture?

Farm machines

There are lots of different machines on the farm, from trucks and tractors to combine harvesters. They all have different jobs to do. Stick them on the road and in the fields.

Find a trailer to add to the back of this tractor.

Find a windmill to add to the picture.

What could you
stick on the road?

The vegetable patch

The vegetables growing here are almost ready to be picked.
Stick some more in the rows and add some tools, too.

Stick on some
more rabbits.

Peas

Carrots

Add some
more signs to label
the vegetables.

Farm store

This store sells some of the things made on the farm.
Fill the shelves with things for sale, from fresh fruits
and vegetables to delicious cheese.

Samples

Put some milk, cheese
and cream in here.

Eggs

County fair

Every year farmers bring their best animals and crops to this county fair. There are competitions to enter and prizes to be won.

Which animal could be stepping out of this trailer?

Put some more stands
inside the food tent.

Give each horse a
ribbon. Who will you
give 1st place to?

Meet the animals

This is where children can feed and pet the animals. Add them all to the picture and see which animal you like the best.

Stick on some children holding animals.

Put some fluffy rabbits in here.

In the farmyard pages 2-3

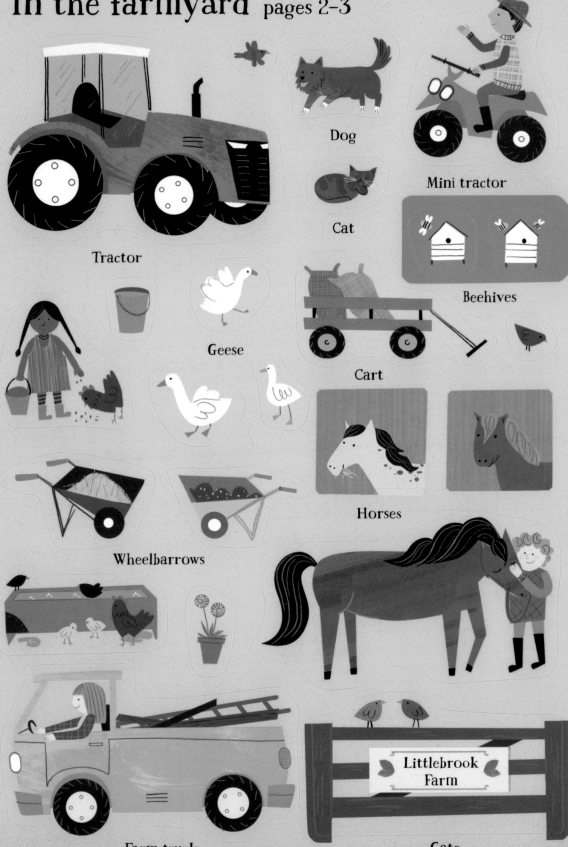

Dog

Mini tractor

Cat

Tractor

Beehives

Geese

Cart

Horses

Wheelbarrows

Farm truck

Littlebrook Farm

Gate

At the cowshed pages 4–5

Cows

Farmer

Goslings

Geese

Calves

Lots of sheep page 6

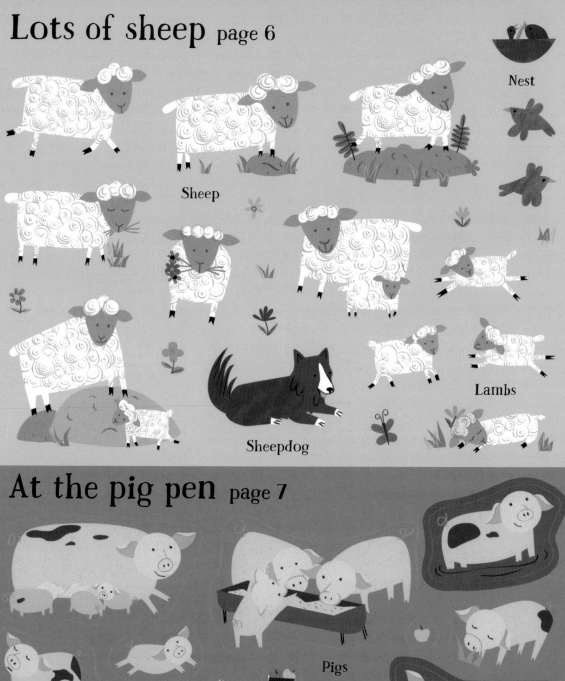

Nest

Sheep

Lambs

Sheepdog

At the pig pen page 7

Pigs

Piglets

At the pond page 8

Frogs

Ducks and ducklings

Lily pad

Goose

Hens and chicks page 9

Chicks

Egg basket

Hen and feeder

Farm machines pages 10–11

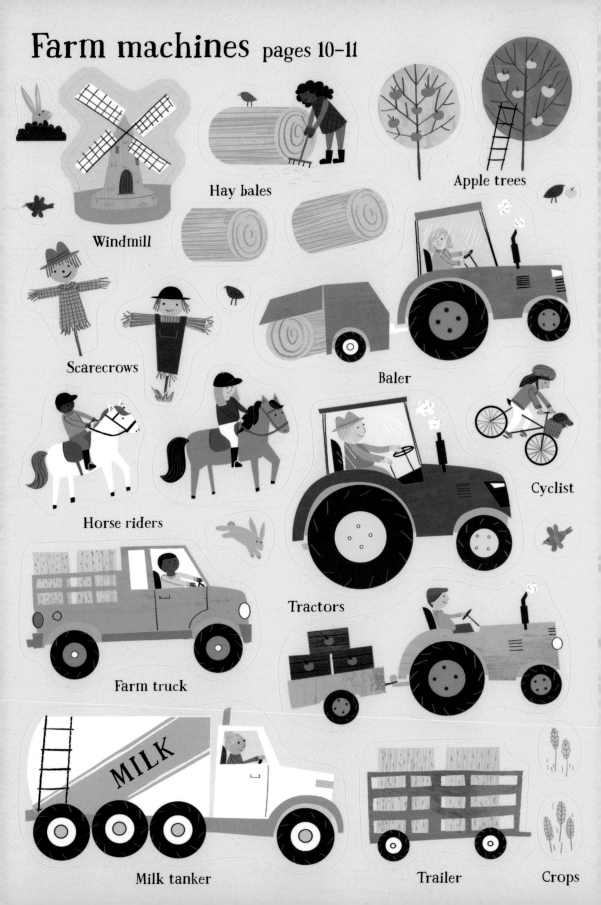

Hay bales

Apple trees

Windmill

Scarecrows

Baler

Horse riders

Cyclist

Tractors

Farm truck

MILK

Milk tanker

Trailer

Crops

The vegetable patch page 12

Cauliflowers

Gardening gloves

Corn

Rabbit

Lettuce

Gardening basket

Farm store page 13

Potatoes

Carrots

Garlic

Honey

Jellies

Milk

Cheese

Cream

Apples

Cake stand

Prize vegetables

Main arena

Food tent

Gloucester Old
Spot pig

Dogs

Alpaca

Ribbons

Highland bull

Food
tent

Wensleydale sheep

Meet the animals page 16

Shetland pony

Ducks

Food

Lamb

Rabbits

Baby goats

Guinea pigs

You can use these stickers anywhere in the book.